PUFFIN BOOKS

MERCEDES ICE

Philip Ridley was born in the East End of London, where he still lives and works. He studied painting at St Martin's School of Art and by the time he graduated had exhibited widely throughout Europe and written his first book. As well as three books for adults, and the highly acclaimed screenplay for *The Krays* feature film, he has written three successful stage plays: *The Pitchfork Disney*, *The Fastest Clock in the Universe* and *Ghost from a Perfect Place*. He has written and directed two films: *The Reflecting Skin* – winner of eleven international awards – and the recently released *The Passion of Darkly Noon*. He has written five other books for children, *Dakota of the White Flats*, *Krindlekrax* (winner of the Smarties Prize and the W.H. Smith Mind-Boggling Books Award), *Meteorite Spoon*, *Kasper in the Glitter* and *Scribbleboy Zing. Kasper in The Glitter* was shortlisted for the 1995 Whitbread Children's Novel of the Year.

Other books by Philip Ridley

DAKOTA OF THE WHITE FLATS
KRINDLEKRAX
METEORITE SPOON
KASPER IN THE GLITTER
SCRIBBLEBOY

For younger readers

DREAMBOAT ZING

Philip Ridley

MERCEDES ICE

An Urban Fairy Story for Modern Children

Illustrated by Chris Riddell

PUFFIN BOOKS

PUFFIN BOOKS

Published by the Penguin Group
Penguin Books Ltd, 27 Wrights Lane, London W8 5TZ, England
Penguin Books USA Inc., 375 Hudson Street, New York, New York 10014, USA
Penguin Books Australia Ltd, Ringwood, Victoria, Australia
Penguin Books Canada Ltd, 10 Alcorn Avenue, Toronto, Ontario, Canada M4V 3B2
Penguin Books (NZ) Ltd, 182–190 Wairau Road, Auckland 10, New Zealand

Penguin Books Ltd, Registered Offices: Harmondsworth, Middlesex, England

First published by William Collins Sons & Co. Ltd 1989
This edition published by Viking 1995
Published in Puffin Books 1996
8

Text copyright © Philip Ridley, 1989
Illustrations copyright © Chris Riddell, 1995
All rights reserved

The moral right of the author has been asserted

Filmset in Palatino

Made and printed in England by Clays Ltd, St Ives plc

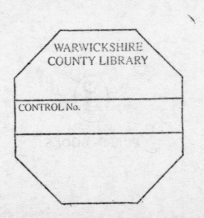

For my brother Tony,
who heard my stories first

Shadow Point wasn't known as Shadow Point from the very beginning. In the early days, when they were still digging the foundations and Rosie was a little girl, it was simply known as the Point. But then, floor by floor, the Point got higher and higher and started to cast a shadow in the streets around it.

Rosie Glow had been born on the first day of Shadow Point.

This is how it happened:

Doll, Rosie's mother, was sitting in her hospital bed. In her arms was the newborn Rosie.

Suddenly the air was full of noises: screeching and roaring like approaching monsters. Birds flew from trees and dogs started to bark.

Rosie cried.

'Hush now,' said Doll, rocking her daughter. 'It's nothing, sweetheart. Nothing.'

But the noises got louder and louder.

Rosie's cries turned to screams.

Doll was worried as well. She had never heard anything like it before. She turned to the woman in the next bed and asked, 'What is it, do you think?'

The woman, a tall, thin, stick of a thing, was holding a baby as well. His name was Timothy.

'Oh, they're digging foundations,' said Timothy's mother. 'Next to the school.'

'Foundations for what?' asked Doll.

'A tower block,' replied Timothy's mother. 'It's going to be the tallest building in the whole area. When it's finished the top will touch the clouds.'

That night, Harold, Doll's husband, came to the hospital to look at Rosie. He gave Doll a bunch of grapes and a pretty card that had 'Well Done' written on it.

Then another man came into the ward. He was tall and muscular and had shining black hair. He walked over to the bed next to Doll and kissed Timothy's mother.

'Dearest!' he exclaimed.

Then he gave Timothy's mother, whose name was Sandra, a brown paper bag.

'This is for you,' he said.

'Thank you,' said Sandra, opening the bag.

Inside were shrimps and shellfish and pickled herring.

Doll pinched her nose and said, 'Oh, what a stink!'

Meanwhile, Timothy's father had picked Timothy up

and was sniffing him all over like a dog sniffs a lamppost.

'Ahhhh, yessssss . . .' he said, between sniffs. 'Halibut . . . Most definitely . . . Halibut . . . I smell halibut without a doubt.'

Later, after the men had gone, Sandra asked Doll, 'What's your baby's full name?'

'Full name?'

'Why, yes. Names are so important, don't you think?'

'Oh, yes. Of course,' said Doll, although the thought had never occurred to her. 'Her name is Rosie Glow.'

Sandra smiled.

'Oh,' she said, 'how interesting. Rosie Glow. How . . . how . . . quaint.' Then she kissed her baby. 'This is my son,' she said softly. 'He's going to be rich and handsome and drive a big expensive car when he grows up.'

'And what's his full name?' asked Doll, because she thought she had to.

'Timothy,' replied Sandra. 'Timothy Ice. I much prefer it to Rosie Glow.' Then she held out the brown paper bag. 'Go on,' she urged. 'Take a shellfish. They're all gritty with sand.'

But Doll hated the smell by now.

The next day Doll took her baby home. On the way they passed the work site where workmen were digging the foundations of Shadow Point.

Doll asked one of the workmen, 'Is it going to be a tall building?'

'Oh yes,' he replied. 'Very tall.'

'Oh dear,' sighed Doll. 'It'll make a big shadow.'

— 2 —

The first place to be cast in this shadow was the school next to the work site.

It was an old school, made out of red brick and plaster. It had a gravel playground that cut your knees to ribbons every time you fell over and a rusty water tap that never worked.

When Rosie was old enough she went to this school. Every day she would stand in the playground and watch the Point getting higher and higher. She even made friends with one of the workmen. His name was Skip and he wore a tin hat painted gold. He was the only one with a hat this colour. All the others were black or white.

'One day,' said Rosie, 'I'm going to live in the Point.'

'Are you now,' chuckled Skip. 'And what floor do you want to be on?'

'How many floors are there going to be?' asked Rosie.

'Thirty-four,' replied Skip.

'Then I'll live on the thirty-fourth floor,' she said. 'The very top.'

'Won't you get giddy?' asked Skip. 'Way up there with nothing to look at but clouds and birds.'

'Oh no,' said Rosie. 'I'd love it. I'll make friends with all the birds and feed them bread and milk.'

Most of the children in the school liked watching the Point being built. And they envied Rosie's friendship with Skip. Sometimes Skip would take Rosie right up to the edge of the work site and let her feel the concrete and metal.

The sight of it thrilled Rosie: the noise, the hustle and bustle, men with dark glasses cutting through steel, sparks and fire, bulldozers digging up clumps of earth big as taxicabs.

Rosie would rush back to the other children and tell them what she had seen. But, because they were jealous, they made out they weren't interested at all and ran away from her.

In the end none of the other children spoke to Rosie and she was left alone. But Rosie wasn't bothered.

'I'll never be alone,' she said. 'Not while I have the Point.'

Rosie's mum, Doll, on the other hand, hated the Point. By now it was eleven floors high and the shadow had reached Doll's house, three streets away.

'It's terrible,' she said to her daughter. 'We don't get any sunlight any more.'

And it was true. All the plants in the window-boxes had turned brown and withered and there were no more flowers in the garden.

'All my plants are dying,' complained Doll. 'What will

we do?'

'When the Point is built,' said Rosie, 'we can move there. If we lived on the top floor we could have all the sunlight we wanted.'

'Never!' cried Doll. 'I'll never move there. This house was my mum's and her mum's before her. I'll never move into that monstrosity.'

But Rosie didn't think it was a monstrosity at all. And she quite liked the shadow it was making. She felt safe and protected in the coolness of the shadow, knowing it had been made by Skip and his mates.

But, one day, while Rosie was in her classroom doing some drawing, there were noises from the work site: a man screaming, then a loud crash, followed by some yells and shouts. Soon afterwards there was an ambulance siren.

The children looked out of the window.

Somebody was being put into the ambulance. The body lay on a stretcher and its face was covered with a white sheet. But Rosie knew who it was. On top of the sheet was a golden tin helmet.

— 3 —

Rosie thought that Skip's death would slow down the building of the Point. But it didn't. Every day Rosie watched it get taller and taller.

When the Point was thirteen floors high a boy came up behind Rosie, tapped her on the shoulder and spoke to her.

'We're the only two,' he said.

He was a pale stick of a boy with short, spiky black hair.

She had been ignored for so long that his friendliness disturbed her.

'The only two what?' she asked.

'Who find it beautiful,' said the boy.

Rosie sniffed.

'What's that smell?' she asked.

'What smell?' asked the boy.

'You smell of the seaside.'

'Do I?' asked the boy. 'Is it nice?'

'No. Not really,' replied Rosie.

There were some loud noises from the building site. A large slab of concrete was fitted into place. Men cheered and clapped.

'Each slab of concrete is a wall,' said Rosie.

'I know,' said the dark-haired boy.

'Four walls make a room, five rooms make a flat, ten flats make a floor and thirty-four floors make the Point.'

'I know,' said the boy.

Rosie stared at him, her eyes wide.

'You do?' she asked him.

'Yes,' he said.

'What's your name?' she asked.

'Tell me yours first,' said the boy.

'Rosie Glow,' said Rosie.

'Timothy Ice,' said the boy. 'Shall we be friends?'

'No,' said Rosie. And walked away.

— 4 —

Day by day the Point got taller and taller. And day by day the shadow got longer and longer.

All around flowers died, grass turned brown and rooms became dark and cold. Old people had to turn on heaters, even in the middle of summer.

'It's just so ugly,' said Doll to Harold as they ate dinner one night. 'Once I used to look out of the window and see trees and flowers, hear singing birds. Now all I see is that ugly grey thing. There're no flowers, no trees, no light, no grass, no birds, nothing.'

'Oh, it's not that bad,' said Harold.

'Don't give me that,' snapped Doll. 'You don't have to watch it. Day in and day out. Watch it getting bigger and bigger and bigger.'

Rosie sat at the table and ate her dinner. She thought her mum was being stupid, although she didn't say so. Instead, she just filled her mouth with a forkful of mashed potato and stared at her plate.

Later, though, while Doll was washing up, Rosie couldn't help saying, '*I* don't think it's ugly.'

'Well, you're as foolish as your father, then.'

'I just think it's . . it's a gigantic finger pointing up to the sky. Or a tall flower. Or a wonderful steeple –'

'Listen, young lady,' interrupted Doll. 'It's not a finger and it's not a flower and it's not a steeple. It's just a shadow. Nothing else. It's just a point of shadow.'

And that was how the Point became known as Shadow Point.

— 5 —

Sometimes it seemed that all Rosie did was watch the building of Shadow Point. She didn't want friends, didn't need her family, had no interest in anything other than Shadow Point.

'You're growing into a lovely girl,' said her mother.

'I'm not lovely at all,' said Rosie.

'We all need a special friend,' said her mother.

'I don't,' said Rosie.

Year by year Shadow Point got taller and taller. And year by year Rosie watched it.

On Rosie's sixteenth birthday two things happened: firstly, Shadow Point reached twenty-seven floors high and, secondly, Rosie's father died.

He came down that morning, gave his daughter a birthday card with a five-pound note inside and said, 'I can't see properly.'

'What do you mean you can't see properly?' asked Doll impatiently.

'Oh, I don't know,' said Harold. 'There're large black blobs in front of my eyes.'

'Large blobs indeed. You've been drinking, haven't you?'

'No,' protested Harold. 'Not a drop. Really. I think I should go back to bed.'

'Back to bed!' cried Doll. 'You get off to work and stop all this moaning. What would happen if I went back to bed every time I had a headache? Now stop being a big baby and get to work.'

Harold got on the bus to go to the factory but he never got there. He died on the bus and his body wasn't discovered until five hours later. By which time he was miles away from home and no one knew who he was.

When his identity was discovered a policeman came to tell Doll. She listened to what he had to say then offered him a cup of tea.

Once he had gone, Doll looked at Rosie and said, 'Trust your father.'

At the funeral Rosie's eyes were fixed on the horizon where she could just make out the top of Shadow Point. It looked dark and wonderful against the light blue sky.

Afterwards, while her mum picked over the funeral flowers with friends and family, Rosie strolled off to wander amongst the gravestones.

There was something about the silence of the graveyard that intrigued her. She had never been anywhere so quiet. She stood still and listened very hard. She was sure she could hear the worms in the earth and ladybirds flying through the air.

Suddenly, she smelt something odd. Something you don't expect to smell in a graveyard.

She looked behind her and saw the black-haired boy standing there. He was eating something from a brown paper bag.

She went over to him and asked, 'Who's buried there?'

'My dad,' he replied.

'I didn't know your dad was dead.'

'I have my secrets,' said the boy.

'What are you eating?' asked Rosie.

Timothy Ice held the bag out and the smell of the seaside got stronger.

The bag was full of cockles and mussels.

'Like one?' asked Timothy.

'No thanks,' replied Rosie, turning away. 'They smell awful.'

'They don't smell at all!' said Timothy.

'Yes they do,' said Rosie.

Timothy looked at the horizon where Shadow Point poked behind the trees.

'Looks beautiful, doesn't it?' he said.

'Seven more floors to go,' said Rosie.

Timothy looked at her and smiled.

'One day I want to live there,' he said softly.

'So do I,' said Rosie.

'Do you?' he asked.

'Oh yes,' she replied. 'The top floor.'

'That's where I want to live. Among the clouds –'

'And the birds!'

'And the planes!'

Rosie looked at him and smiled.

'I think I'll have something to eat now,' she said. And took a cockle from his brown paper bag.

'What are you doing in a graveyard anyway?' he asked.

'My dad's funeral,' she replied.

'I didn't know he had died,' said Timothy.

'I have my secrets too,' said Rosie.

'Shall we be friends?' asked Timothy.

'Mmn,' said Rosie, chewing a cockle.

— 6 —

After the funeral Rosie went round to Timothy's house. It was a tiny flat in a dingy street. The street was just being touched by the shadow of Shadow Point.

'Three more floors,' said Timothy, 'that's all it will take. Then my flat will be completely in the shadow.'

'Let me see,' said Rosie thoughtfully. 'That will take about . . . another two years.'

'That's right,' said Timothy.

Timothy's mother, Sandra, was still tall and thin. She was dressed in black. She said hello to Rosie then made a pot of tea and some salmon sandwiches.

'My husband was the most handsome man in the world,' said Sandra, sitting at the table opposite Rosie and Timothy. 'He brought me presents of shrimps and starfish the colour of fire. Every week he gave me a beautiful shell because he loved me so much. Would you like to see them, Rosie?'

Rosie didn't want to see them at all but felt that she had to.

'Oh yes,' said Rosie politely. 'Please. I'd love to see your shells.'

Sandra took Rosie to her bedroom and flicked on the light. The room was full of all kinds of shells; they were stuck to the walls and covered the ceiling; there were ashtrays made out of shells, fruit bowls, earrings, necklaces, brooches, flowerpots, tables, chairs, jewel boxes, everything made out of shells, shells of all sizes and colours.

Rosie's mouth dropped open in wonder. She hadn't expected the room to look so beautiful. It shimmered with its ghostly treasure.

'You like it?' asked Sandra.

'Oh yes,' said Rosie. 'Very much.'

'A lifetime of love is in this room,' said Sandra. 'My husband gave me all the prettiest things.'

Then Sandra reached under the bed and pulled out something Rosie had never seen before. It was huge and white and very scary. It looked like two gigantic chicken wishbones stuck together.

'You know what this is?' asked Sandra.

Rosie shook her head.

'It's the jaws of a shark,' said Sandra gleefully. 'My husband travelled to some pretty islands when he was a young man. There – in an ocean so clear you could see the shipwrecks on the sea bed – he killed this shark with his bare hands. Then he brought me back these jaws. Brought them back just for me. They were his wedding present, you know.'

'They're incredible,' said Rosie.

'When *you* get married,' said Sandra, bringing her lips close to Rosie's ear, 'make sure your husband gives you a gift as special as this.'

'I will,' said Rosie. 'I will.'

At that moment Timothy came into the room. His black hair looked even blacker against the luminous whiteness of the seashells.

'This room gives me a headache,' he moaned.

Sandra looked at her son and said, 'Take Rosie home, Timothy. There's a good boy.'

As Timothy walked her home, Rosie grabbed hold of his arm and said, 'You should leave school and get a job.'

'Why?' asked Timothy.

'So you can save lots of money,' said Rosie, thinking of a flat in Shadow Point.

— 7 —

The next day Timothy left school and started work on the seafood stall that had belonged to his father and grandfather.

He wore a spotless white overall and called everyone 'mate' or 'luv'. He became very popular in the market. People said he was 'a real character'.

Rosie spent all her spare time at the stall with Timothy, watching him chop up eels and clean fish. His hands were so quick and beautiful that every time she looked at him she wanted to cry.

'Seafood will make me rich,' said Timothy. 'And I want to save all the money I can.'

'Why?' asked Rosie.

'To buy a car,' he replied.

'And that's all?'

'Oh, not just any car,' said Timothy.

'What kind of car then?' asked Rosie.

'I'm going to get a Mercedes,' replied Timothy. And his eyes sparkled with wonder.

'What's a Mercedes?' asked Rosie.

'It's the most beautiful thing in the world,' said Timothy. 'It's black and shining and lethal. Like a living chunk of black ice. If I had one of those I'd be perfectly happy.'

All this worried Rosie. She tugged at his white sleeve and plucked fluff from his lapel.

'But I thought you wanted to live in Shadow Point more than anything else in the world,' she said.

'Oh, I do,' said Timothy eagerly, 'I do. But I want a car as well. A person can want more than one thing, can't they?'

'I don't think so,' said Rosie sulkily. 'All I want to do is live at the very top of Shadow Point. If I could do that then I'd be perfectly happy.'

'Then we will,' said Timothy.

'Both of us?' asked Rosie.

'Both of us.'

'Together?'

'Together.'

And they kissed each other.

When Rosie got back home her mother sniffed her.

'What's wrong with you?' asked Rosie.

'You're seeing that boy, aren't you?' accused Doll.

'What boy?' asked Rosie.

'Don't play games with me. I'd know that smell anywhere. That Timothy Ice, Sandra Ice's boy.'

'What if I am seeing him?' asked Rosie.

'He's not good enough, that's what,' said Doll, stamp-
ing her foot. 'All he wants to do is work on that smelly
seafood stall just like his father. He might be good-looking
but that's not everything.'

'*Is* he good-looking?' asked Rosie.

'Well, don't *you* think so?'

'I don't know,' said Rosie.

'Then why are you seeing him?' asked Doll.

Rosie thought for a while. The question had never really
occurred to her before.

'Because . . . because he's the only one there,' she said.

'Hardly a reason to go out with him,' commented Doll.

'Why did you go out with Dad?' asked Rosie.

'Because he made me laugh,' said Doll.

Rosie frowned. She couldn't imagine her father ever making anyone laugh.

Doll noticed her daughter's expression.

'In the beginning,' said Doll, 'your father was very funny. He told the best jokes I'd ever heard. But then . . . then he lost it.'

'Where did it go?' asked Rosie.

'I don't know,' answered Doll. 'I just woke up one morning and found this grey, humourless man beside me.'

And Doll started to cry. Large tears trickled down her cheeks and off the end of her chin. It was the first time Rosie had seen her mother cry and it scared her. She hugged her mother.

'Don't let it happen to you,' sobbed Doll. 'Don't let it happen to you.'

Rosie kissed her mother.

'Don't worry,' she said. 'I won't.'

— 8 —

As soon as she could, Rosie left school and went to work in the local cake shop. She loved to look at all the different pastries. Her favourite was the rum baba. It smelt exotic and was a lovely rust colour.

All the customers liked Rosie because she was cheerful and knew all there was to know about the different cakes.

Timothy's favourite cake was called a vanilla slice. He always ate one with a cup of tea. He liked the way the yellow cream squeezed from between the slices of pastry when he bit into it.

'You'll get fat,' warned Rosie.

'I don't care,' said Timothy, biting into another vanilla slice. 'You're getting fat too.'

Rosie and Timothy giggled and hugged each other; vanilla cream from Timothy's lips got on Rosie's lips and rum from Rosie's lips got on Timothy's lips.

'You taste nice,' said Rosie.

'So do you,' said Timothy.

Timothy bought Rosie a golden ring, and Rosie bought Timothy a golden ring. They got married as soon as they could. And, as chance would have it, the day Rosie and Timothy got married was the day the workmen finished building Shadow Point.

The wedding was wet and crowded.

All the people who worked in the cake shop were there, and all the people who knew Timothy from the market were there.

Rosie wore white and Timothy wore black. Everyone said what a beautiful couple they made, even if Rosie was getting a little plump.

'It's all those cakes,' said Doll. 'Working in the shop, she just stuffs her face all day.'

Timothy's mother, Sandra, was there. She wore a peach-coloured, two-piece suit and a hat so big it made her look like a mushroom.

Sandra said to Rosie, 'Now then, Rosie, has my son bought you something as impressive as my shark jaws?'

'Oh yes,' replied Rosie.

'What?'

'He's got me a flat at the top of Shadow Point.'

Sandra frowned and touched the white veil Rosie was wearing.

'Is that enough?' she said.

'Yes,' said Rosie. 'I think so.'

Later, after the wedding, Rosie noticed that her mother, Doll, was crying.

'Don't cry, Mum,' said Rosie.

'I can't help it,' sobbed Doll. 'He's not good enough for you. You know that.'

'But I love him, Mum,' said Rosie.

'You don't love him. You don't know what love is. Oh, I can't bear it. You'll always smell of haddock and lobsters now. That awful smell.' Doll sniffed. 'I can smell him from here. Even in a new suit he reeks of seaweed.'

Rosie sniffed as hard as she could.

'Well, I can't smell anything,' she said.

'Of course not,' snapped Doll. 'Because you stink of it too.'

Rosie clutched her mother's hand.

'Oh, don't be like this, Mum,' she pleaded. 'No matter what I smell like I'm still your little Rosie, aren't I?'

'No,' said Doll, 'you're not. Not any more. From now on you've lost your real name. It's gone for ever. You're no longer my little Rosie Glow. From now on you're just Mrs Ice.'

Rosie shivered when she heard the name. She let go of her mother's hand.

'I know,' said Rosie quietly. 'I'm Mrs Ice.'

— 9 —

In the beginning Shadow Point might have been considered beautiful. Certainly Rosie – now Mrs Ice – thought so. She loved the smooth, grey concrete and the big windows and the silver gleam of the television aerials.

She lived on the very top floor with Timothy. Every morning she would get up and look at the clouds and birds. She could see for miles and miles right across the city. For her, it was all magical and wonderful and she was perfectly happy.

That was in the beginning. But things didn't last. Because, whatever beauty Shadow Point might have had, it soon faded.

Before long the smooth, grey concrete became buckled and discoloured. The big windows were impossible to clean so they became thick with dust and let no light in. The silver gleam of the television aerials soon became a rusty forest on the roof of the building, like a gigantic bird's nest.

Shadow Point became dark. Hundreds of pigeons and sparrows made their homes in the maze of television aerials. Before long, thousands of birds were squawking and screaming around Shadow Point. The bird droppings stuck to the side of the building and turned green and hard. Soon Shadow Point began to change shape. It started to resemble a mountain rising bleak and menacing above the rooftops.

— 10 —

'It's driving me mad,' said Rosie – now Mrs Ice – to Timothy. 'All day long I can hear nothing but the sound of birds and the screaming of children from the school yard next door. It's driving me mad!'

'You went to that school once,' Timothy reminded her.

'I never made a noise like that,' protested Mrs Ice – who was once Rosie.

'I bet you did,' said Timothy.

'I tell you I didn't. And even if I did, there weren't people living right next door then. Oh, it's disgraceful! I hate the noise, Timothy! Really I do!'

'It was your idea to live here,' said Timothy.

'It was your idea as well,' said Mrs Ice, once Rosie.

'Was it?' remarked Timothy. 'I forget now.'

Mrs Ice felt very alone. Not only had her own mother died, but Sandra Ice, Timothy's mother, had died as well. Sandra had choked on a cockle, and Doll had been knocked down by a double-decker bus. As if this wasn't enough, Mrs Ice realized that she didn't like living in Shadow Point any more. If she thought about it carefully she realized that Timothy wasn't the same as he was before. To begin with, his hair was falling out. Every time Mrs Ice went to the sink she found long black hairs clogging up the plughole.

She showed her husband the hairs one day.

'You're going bald!' she accused him.

'No I'm not,' he protested.

'But . . . just look at these hairs.'

'Listen!' he said. 'I'm not going bald.'

Mrs Ice ran over to her husband and ran her fingers through his hair.

'There!' she exclaimed triumphantly. 'You've got a bald patch! Look!'

Carefully, Timothy rearranged his hair to conceal his bald patch once again. Then he looked up at Mrs Ice and said, 'No I haven't.'

But, every day, more and more hair fell out and the bald patch got bigger and bigger.

And that wasn't all that irritated Mrs Ice.

The other thing was cars.

All day long Timothy talked about cars. Cars, cars, cars. He made a few friends. And all they talked about was cars. Cars, cars, cars.

'I can't stand it!' said Mrs Ice. 'If you love cars so much why don't you just buy one?'

'Because we can't afford it!' said Timothy.

'Then you should work harder at the stall,' said Mrs Ice.

'Oh, I'm thinking about selling that,' said Timothy. 'I'm going to sell it and buy a garage instead.'

Mrs Ice was flabbergasted.

'The seafood stall has been in your family for years,' she said. 'You can't sell it!'

'I can if I want to,' said Timothy.

'Your mum will turn in her grave,' said Mrs Ice.

At that moment all the seashells that Timothy's mother had left him started to shake and rattle. The seashells were all over the flat now and Mrs Ice had grown to love them. Some of the shells shook so much they cracked open. Also, the gigantic shark jaws started to snap open and shut as if they wanted to eat Timothy.

'All right!' screamed Timothy, afraid now. 'All right! I won't buy a garage. I'll run the seafood stall all my life.'

As soon as he said this, the shells stopped shaking and the jaws stopped snapping.

Mrs Ice looked at her husband and smiled.

'You see!' she said. 'The ghosts are on my side! Anyway, you can't risk changing your job at the moment.'

'Why not?' asked Timothy.

'We're going to have a baby,' said Mrs Ice.

'How do *you* know?' asked Timothy.

'The doctor told me.'

'And how does *he* know?' asked Timothy.

'Because he's a doctor,' said Mrs Ice. 'And, anyway, what's wrong? I thought you'd be pleased.'

'Oh . . . I am pleased,' said Timothy softly. 'It's just that . . . well . . . I wanted a car first. I wanted to buy my gleaming Mercedes.'

Mrs Ice kissed her husband's bald patch and said, 'You can't have everything.'

'But I don't want everything,' said Timothy. 'I just want a car.'

— 11 —

Shadow Point continued to get uglier by the day.

Whole walls fell out and were replaced with corrugated iron, windows broke and were replaced with hardboard, doors split open and were covered with metal grids. Abandoned cars started to pile up around the base of Shadow Point. Rats made their homes in these cars. The rats were vicious and spiteful. People became afraid to go near Shadow Point in case they were attacked or bitten.

The strangest thing of all was the fact that Mrs Ice never met any of the other people living in Shadow Point. She knew that they were there but she never saw them. Sometimes she stood for hours on the stairs, yearning for someone to talk to. But, although she heard footsteps and voices, she never saw the people they belonged to.

For most of the day, she did the housework and watched the television. She still worked at the cake shop. But part time now.

When she wasn't doing the housework or watching television, she was eating. She liked the other cakes as well as the rum babas now. Anything with fresh cream was her favourite. As a result, she got fatter and fatter. None of her clothes would fit her any more so she had to buy some new ones.

'We can't afford new clothes!' said Timothy.

'But nothing fits me any more,' said Mrs Ice.

'Just stop eating.'

'*You* can talk. You're getting fat too.'

'No I'm not.'

Mrs Ice grabbed a tape-measure and wrapped it round her husband's waist.

'There you are!' she cried. 'Fifty inches! You had a twenty-eight-inch waist when I first married you.'

'Well, it's different for me,' said Timothy. 'I'm eating seafood. And that's healthy for you. You're just stuffing your face with cakes and pastries.'

'You'll have a heart attack,' said Mrs Ice.

'No I won't,' said Timothy.

But he did . . .

— 12 —

Coming home from work one evening, Timothy heard a noise. It was a dark, cold night and the noise came from amongst the cars piled high around Shadow Point.

Timothy looked into the buckled wreckage of the cars. 'Who's there?' he asked.

But no answer came.

He walked a few steps further on.

The noise came again.

Timothy spun round . . .

Behind him was a gigantic rat. It was a monstrous, hairy thing with eyes like red traffic lights, sharp yellow teeth and a long pink tail like a fat worm.

The rat was sniffing Timothy.

'Help!' cried Timothy. 'Help!'

But no help came. There were lots of screams at night in Shadow Point and no one took any notice of them any more.

'Help!' he cried again. 'Help!'

He pressed the button to call the lift but the lift was on the top floor and would take ages to get to him.

In desperation he started to run up the icy cold, concrete steps.

For a second he thought he was safe.

But he wasn't!

Still the rat chased after him!

Sweat started to trickle down Timothy's back and his heart started to pound.

'Help!'

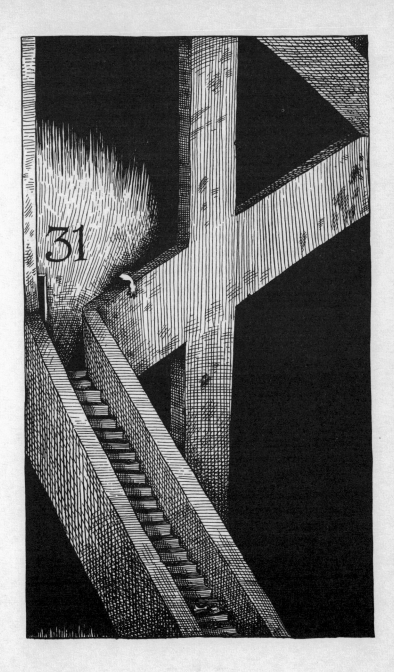

But his voice was fainter now, barely loud enough to echo down the cavernous stairs.

Behind him, Timothy could hear the scraping of the rat's clawed feet.

By the time he reached the twenty-fourth floor Timothy was exhausted.

By the twenty-fifth he felt faint and giddy.

By the twenty-sixth he couldn't breathe.

By the twenty-eighth his legs started to give way.

By the twenty-ninth he started to have a heart attack.

By the thirtieth he was having a heart attack.

Timothy finally died on the thirty-first floor.

The rat had given up chasing him on the twenty-third floor. But Timothy never knew that.

Mrs Ice told the police that Timothy was missing and the police carried out a search. But they never looked on the stairs.

The body was finally found by a small, bird-like woman.

It was this woman who told the police.

And it was this woman who consoled Mrs Ice and helped her with all the funeral arrangements.

'He was such a gentle man,' said Mrs Ice. 'He didn't want anything. Well, just a car.'

'Most men don't,' said the woman.

Mrs Ice smiled and hugged the woman.

'You know,' said Mrs Ice, 'you're the first friend I've made since I came to live at Shadow Point.'

'And you're the first friend I've made,' said the woman.

'I'm going to be a mother soon,' said Mrs Ice.

'So am I,' said the woman.

'And I haven't got a husband,' said Mrs Ice.

'Neither have I,' said the woman.

Mrs Ice looked at the woman and smiled.

'What's your name?' asked Mrs Ice.

'Hilda Sparkle,' said the woman.

— 13 —

Hilda Sparkle lived on the same floor as Mrs Ice. Every day the women got together to drink tea and eat the pastries Mrs Ice brought home from the cake shop.

Mrs Ice was still getting fatter and fatter. In fact, it was sometimes difficult for her to get through the front door and she could no longer sit down in the bath.

'You'll just have to lose weight,' said Hilda.

'But you eat just as much as I do,' said Mrs Ice. 'Why don't you put on weight?'

'I don't know,' said Hilda. 'I just don't.'

'All right, then,' said Mrs Ice, feeling her flab. 'I'll try to get thinner.'

But the more she tried to lose weight, the more she ate. She just got fatter and fatter and fatter.

'It's not that you eat too much,' explained Hilda. 'It's just that you eat all the wrong things.'

'I know,' agreed Mrs Ice. 'But if it's there, I just have to eat it. Some nights I wake up and I'm so hungry that I get through ten rum babas, five chocolate éclairs and seven custard tarts in five and a half minutes.'

'Well, that's terrible,' said Hilda. 'I'll tell you what we'll do. This evening we're going to take all your cakes and put them in my flat.'

'Oh, what a good idea,' said Mrs Ice.

And that's what they did.

It took them over three hours to get all the cakes into Hilda Sparkle's flat.

'Now, you go home,' said Hilda, 'and think of other

things. Watch the television, do the crossword, anything.
Just don't think about food.'

So Mrs Ice went back to her flat and closed the door.
First, she sat down in front of the television and watched
her favourite programme. But everyone in the programme seemed to be eating, so that was no good. Next,
Mrs Ice looked out the window. Thousands of birds
swooped and swarmed around the top of Shadow Point,
and all the birds had either worms or beetles in their
beaks. Mrs Ice was so hungry by now that even the worms
and beetles looked tempting.

That night she didn't sleep at all. The sound of her
rumbling stomach kept her awake. All she could think of
were rum babas and chocolate éclairs and custard tarts.

Suddenly Mrs Ice couldn't stand it any longer. She got
to her feet and ran out of her flat. She knocked down

Hilda's door with one heave of her massive, starving shoulder.

Her eyes glaring, Mrs Ice started to rip Hilda's flat apart. She tore shelves from walls, ripped off cupboard doors and pulled up the carpets.

'Where are they?' she screamed. 'Where are my rum babas?'

The noise woke Hilda. She jumped out of bed and tried to restrain Mrs Ice.

'Don't!' cried Hilda. 'Don't!'

Mrs Ice was in Hilda's bedroom. She tugged the sheets from the bed.

'I want my rum babas!' she screamed.

Then she opened the wardrobe door.

And stopped.

Stopped dead in her tracks and did not move.

Her mouth dropped open and she forgot all about her hunger. Inside the wardrobe was something that made her feel faint. All she could do was stare at it.

Hilda came up behind her.

'What's wrong?' she asked.

Mrs Ice continued to stare.

'Oh, that,' said Hilda, following her gaze. 'That belonged to my father. He was one of the workmen that helped build Shadow Point. He was killed by a falling piece of concrete.'

Mrs Ice reached out and took the golden tin helmet from the wardrobe.

'His name was Skip,' said Hilda softly.

Mrs Ice gave a little scream.

'Are you still hungry?' asked Hilda.

'No,' said Mrs Ice. 'I'm going to have my baby.'

Hilda helped Mrs Ice back to her flat. She put her to bed, then called for the doctor.

But the baby was born before the doctor arrived.

— 14 —

It was a boy. He was born with a mass of black hair. His eyes were large and dark and his lips as red as blood.

'Looks like a little monster,' said Hilda.

'Just like his father,' said Mrs Ice.

'What are you going to call him?' asked Hilda.

'Well,' said Mrs Ice thoughtfully, 'his father always

wanted a car. But he never got one. Now . . . what was the car my husband always wanted? It . . . it had a strange name . . . what was it now?'

'Mini?' suggested Hilda.

'No,' said Mrs Ice.

'Jaguar?' offered Hilda.

'No,' said Mrs Ice. Then she remembered. 'I know what it was. It was a . . . a Mercedes.' And she spelt the name out loud: 'M-E-R-C-E-D-E-S.'

Hilda smiled and kissed the baby.

'Welcome, Mercedes Ice,' she said.

Later that night, when it was dark and the whole of Shadow Point was asleep, Mrs Ice wrapped Mercedes in a blanket and took him to the roof.

It was cold and breezy up there.

Mrs Ice made her way through the forest of television aerials until she could see a patch of sky. It was a clear night and the sky was sparkling with millions of stars and one big, bright skull of a moon.

All round her, thousands of birds slept.

Mrs Ice lifted her son into the air.

'You are Mercedes Ice,' she said. 'You will be special and wonderful and magical. This is Shadow Point, your kingdom. You are now the Prince of Shadow Point and everything you want will be yours. This is your world.'

Then she kissed her son.

The baby's tiny eyes opened and he smiled at her.

Then Mrs Ice screamed his name as loud as she could: 'MERCEDES ICE!'

Immediately, the birds awoke and erupted in flight around her. They swarmed around the top of Shadow Point like a million moths around a flame.

The flapping of their wings was deafening. They rained a storm of feathers down on Mrs Ice and Mercedes. There were so many birds they blocked out the sky. It became quite dark, the darkest it had ever been in the kingdom of Shadow Point.

— 15 —

Mercedes grew to be a very special child. He could talk by the time he was one year old, read and write by the time he was two and draw beautiful pictures by the time he was three. Mrs Ice was so very proud of her son. He was everything to her. She bought him the most expensive pram she could find. It was big and silver with a shiny black hood.

Unfortunately, though, the pram was never used,

because, although Mrs Ice no longer ate rum babas, the skin round her stomach had stretched so much that she couldn't get through the front door. So Mrs Ice was trapped in her flat at Shadow Point. But Mrs Ice didn't mind. She had her baby and her baby was special and wonderful and that's all that mattered.

Hilda did the shopping for Mrs Ice. Hilda had her own baby now. It was a beautiful blonde girl with grey eyes. Hilda named the child Hickory.

'Why Hickory?' asked Mrs Ice.

'Because I intend to have three children,' said Hilda. 'The first one is Hickory, then the next two I will call Dickory and Dock.'

'Hickory, Dickory, Dock,' said Mrs Ice.

'That's right,' said Hilda, and smiled. 'What do you think?'

'I think it sounds perfect,' replied Mrs Ice.

'And what about you?' asked Hilda. 'Do you want more children?'

'Oh no,' said Mrs Ice. 'I only want the one. My Mercedes is everything to me. I'll do anything for him.'

And she did. Right from the very beginning, anything Mercedes wanted, he got. Mrs Ice had a lot of money from the sale of Timothy's seafood stall and she spent nearly all of it on Mercedes. She gave him the money for a gleaming silver bicycle, roller skates, a toy robot, a kite, a doll and a doll's house, a very difficult puzzle and all the sweets and chocolates he could eat.

But still it wasn't enough.

Mercedes wanted more.

Because Mrs Ice was too big and flabby to leave the flat, she lost contact with all her friends from the cake shop. Hilda was worried that Mrs Ice was lonely.

'Not at all,' said Mrs Ice. 'I have Mercedes now.'

As soon as he was old enough to walk and talk, Mercedes had made friends with Hilda's daughter, Hickory Sparkle.

Hickory was fascinated by Mercedes, mainly because he had so many toys and sweets.

'If you become my best friend,' said Mercedes, 'I'll give you a bar of chocolate.'

'I am your best friend,' said Hickory.

So Mercedes gave her a bar of chocolate.

'If you'll be my best friend for ever and ever and ever,' said Mercedes, 'I'll give you an apple dipped in sticky golden toffee.'

'I'll be your best friend for ever and ever and ever,' said Hickory.

So Mercedes gave her an apple dipped in sticky golden toffee.

And so it went on.

But Mercedes had no need to buy Hickory's friendship. She adored him anyway. She thought he was the greatest thing alive.

Mercedes grew to know Shadow Point like the back of his hand. He knew every crack in the concrete, every smashed window, every hole in the floorboards, all the places where rats made their homes and birds made their nests. He loved every square inch of Shadow Point. But his favourite place of all was the roof.

One day he took Hickory up there.

'This is the top of my kingdom,' he said. 'There are a million, million birds up here. They make their nests in the television aerials and wash in the puddles. They feed their children on worms and bits of food from the rubbish scattered around my kingdom.'

Hickory looked round her and was not impressed.

'The basement is better,' she said.

'The basement?' said Mercedes.

'Yes,' said Hickory. 'It's full of spiders and cockroaches and all sorts of bug-like things. I've made friends with them all. The spiders make huge cobwebs just for me.'

'Well, of course, I like the basement,' said Mercedes. 'It's part of my kingdom. But my favourite place is still the roof.' Then he looked at Hickory and smiled. 'I know what I'll do,' he said. 'I'll give you the basement as a gift. That will be your own little island within my kingdom. And I name you . . . the Cobweb Princess.'

Hickory tingled all over.

'Oh, thank you,' she said. 'Thank you.'

And she kissed the Prince of Shadow Point.

— 16 —

Later that day Hickory went down to the basement. It was dark and damp and the air shook with the buzz from the gigantic boilers.

The basement was a maze of rusty pipes and tubes. Hickory knew every nook and cranny of the place. She stood in the middle of the basement and she felt it hum and shake around her.

Then she went over to the corner where she knew the biggest spiders were. Carefully, she scooped up all the spiders' webs she could find and stuck them to her back so that they resembled a magnificent cloak.

The next morning Hickory went to the roof and showed Mercedes what she had made.

'What do you think?' she asked.

Mercedes shrugged and looked the other way.

'Not bad,' he murmured.

But – secretly – he thought it was the most beautiful thing he had ever seen. He was so jealous he felt sick to the stomach and he couldn't even look at Hickory.

'Go away,' he said. 'I don't feel very well.'

Tears appeared in Hickory's eyes.

'But, Mercedes . . .' she said softly, touching his arm.

Mercedes pulled away.

'Don't touch me!' he said. 'Go away! This is my special part of the kingdom and you don't belong up here when you're wearing your cloak.'

So, still in tears, Hickory ran away.

Mercedes went straight to Mrs Ice and started hugging her.

'Oh, Mummy,' he said. 'Dearest, sweetest, kindest of all mummies.'

'What is it, sweetheart?' asked Mrs Ice.

'That girl,' he said. 'That Hickory Sparkle. She's got a cloak made out of cobwebs. And it's more beautiful than anything I've got.'

Mrs Ice cuddled Mercedes.

'What do you want me to do, darling?' she asked.

'I want . . .' Mercedes answered thoughtfully. 'I want a cloak as well. I want the most beautiful cloak ever made.'

Mrs Ice was aghast.

'But what – what shall I make this cloak out of?' she asked.

'Rat skins,' answered Mercedes.

'Well,' said Mrs Ice, 'if you want it . . . you shall have it. I'll do anything for you, you know that.'

So Mercedes bought his mother a fishing-rod, and, every day, Mrs Ice stuck a piece of cheese on to the fishing-hook and let it down the whole length of Shadow Point until it reached the wrecked cars below. And then, one at a time, she would catch the rats on the fishing-hook and haul them all the way up to her flat on the thirty-fourth floor.

It took her five weeks to catch all the rats she needed. At the end of the five weeks she carefully sewed all the rat skins together and presented Mercedes with his cloak.

Mercedes went straight to the roof.

The cloak was perfect.

When he was sure that he looked wonderful he called Hickory up from her basement to see him.

'You see,' said Mercedes, 'I look much better than you do.'

'Yes,' said Hickory, 'you do.'

When Hickory went back to the basement she threw away her beloved cobweb cloak. She realized that she must never look better than Mercedes Ice. Only then would he be happy and be her friend.

Meanwhile, back on the roof, Mercedes said, 'I'm pleased with the cloak. But it's not enough.'

And then he screamed, 'I WANT MORE! I WANT MORE! I WANT MORE!'

As his voice echoed down to Hickory in the basement she started to cry. She rushed back to her flat. Her mother asked her what was wrong. Hickory wouldn't say.

'Is it that Mercedes again?' asked Hilda.

Hickory nodded.

Angry, Hilda went to see Mrs Ice.

'Your son's a menace,' she said. 'He bosses my daughter around and he bosses you around. And it's all your fault.'

'Why is it my fault?' asked Mrs Ice.

'Because you're spoiling him,' said Hilda angrily. 'You give him everything he wants. It's not right. You're turning him into a monster.'

'My son's not a monster, he's a little angel,' cried Mrs Ice.

'But –'

'Go!' cried Mrs Ice. 'I never want to see you again.'

'Don't be stupid,' said Hilda patiently. 'Who'll buy your food? You'd starve to death if it wasn't for me.'

'Mercedes will shop for me,' said Mrs Ice.

'You're a bigger fool than I thought if you imagine Mercedes will lift one finger to help you or anyone.'

'I never want to see you again!' cried Mrs Ice.

And that was how Mrs Ice stopped speaking to Hilda.

Meanwhile, Mercedes had fallen asleep on the roof.

Five hours later he woke up.

Everything around him was white.

A white landscape with black buildings.

Black birds flying across a white sky.

Mercedes stood up and looked all round him.

All he could see was black and white, black and white, black and white.

'The world,' he whispered. 'The world has turned black and white.'

Mercedes went to Mrs Ice.

'Where's all the colour gone?' asked Mercedes.

'What do you mean, darling?' she asked.

'All the wonderful colours!' cried Mercedes. 'All the reds and yellows and greens and blues. There's nothing left. Nothing. Everything is colourless!'

'It's just been snowing, darling,' said Mrs Ice. 'That's all.'

She went to hug her son, but he pushed her away and started to cry.

'I want something colourful!' cried Mercedes. 'I want something colourful! I want something colourful!'

And Mrs Ice sighed and frowned and wondered what she could do.

'I'm going to bed!' exclaimed Mercedes. 'And I'm not getting up until I have something that is colourful! Something that . . . that I can wear! Something that will make me stand out in the crowd! Something that will make me look better than everyone else! Do you hear me?'

'Yes, darling,' said Mrs Ice softly.

— 18 —

The day after Mercedes took to his bed it was Hilda's birthday. She knew it was her birthday, because she received a card from a friend she had known many, many years ago.

'Well, well, well,' said Hilda, sitting in her kitchen and looking at the card. 'I'm getting old.'

At that moment Hickory came in and asked why her mother looked so sad.

'Because it's my birthday,' explained Hilda, 'and I'm not the same as I was before.'

When she heard this, Hickory's face went bright red, not because her mother was getting old, but because she had forgotten it was her birthday and she hadn't bought her a present.

So, instantly, Hickory put on her big, warm coat and boots, because it was still thick with snow outside, and rushed to the nearby market to buy Hilda a gift.

Hickory searched the market for hours but couldn't find a suitable present. Nothing seemed right somehow. Her mother was so difficult to please.

Then she glanced in a shop window and saw something so bright and colourful it made her eyes water. It was a bird with bright yellow feathers and a small orange beak. Hickory had never seen anything so dazzling. It was like a chirping handful of sunlight.

She went into the shop and bought the bird. The shopkeeper put the bird in a white cardboard box and put two elastic bands round it.

Then Hickory ran back to Shadow Point and gave it to her mother.

Hilda cried when she saw it.

'Oh, it's so beautiful,' she said. 'So very beautiful.'

And she kissed the hard beak of the yellow bird.

'I'm glad you like it,' said Hickory. 'Now I've got to go.'

'Where?' asked Hilda.

'To Mrs Ice,' said Hickory. 'I've got her some cakes.'

Because Hilda no longer spoke to Mrs Ice and Mercedes would never go shopping, it was up to Hickory to get food so that Mrs Ice and her son wouldn't starve.

She rushed to Mrs Ice's flat and put some rum babas on the kitchen table. As she did so she heard Mercedes crying in his bedroom.

'What's wrong with him?' she asked.

'Oh, you know what he's like,' said Mrs Ice, taking a bite from the biggest cake she could find. 'Always wanting, wanting. He says the world has turned black and

white and he's going to stay in bed until he has something
colourful to wear. He won't believe me when I tell him it's
just snow and it'll soon melt.'

'Can I see him?' asked Hickory.

'If you like,' replied Mrs Ice.

Hickory knocked on Mercedes's bedroom door and
went inside.

Mercedes was sitting up in bed with a plate of biscuits in
front of him. The sheets were covered in crumbs and bits
of burnt toast.

Hickory pinched her nose and said, 'It stinks in here!'

'No it doesn't,' said Mercedes.

'That's because you stink too,' said Hickory.

'If you don't like it, go away,' said Mercedes.

'Why are you in bed, anyway?'

'Because everything is ugly.'

'Am I ugly?'

'Yes,' said Mercedes. 'Very ugly.'

'And what about you?' asked Hickory. 'Are you ugly too?'

'Oh, I *feel* it,' said Mercedes. 'I feel it without something colourful to wear.'

There were tears in Hickory's eyes now.

Mercedes was her friend. There was no one else in the whole of Shadow Point who played with her. She loved Mercedes and missed him. She wanted him to get out of bed and be her friend again.

'If I bring you something,' said Hickory softly, 'something that has colour, will you get up?'

'I might do,' replied Mercedes. 'You'll just have to find out.'

So Hickory rushed back to her flat and plucked a feather from the yellow bird. Then she rushed back to Mercedes and showed it to him.

At once his eyes lit up and he held the feather as if it were a precious diamond or ruby.

'It has colour!' he cried. 'It is something yellow! It's the most wonderful thing I've seen. I need all the other feathers. I . . . I have to have the bird.'

'But my mother loves the bird,' explained Hickory. 'If I take the bird away from her it will upset her.'

'I don't care!' cried Mercedes. 'Let her be upset! I want the bird. I need the bird. I have to have the bird.'

'If . . . if I get you the bird,' said Hickory, staring into Mercedes's eyes, 'will you love me?'

'I don't know,' said Mercedes. 'You'll just have to find out.'

— 19 —

That night Hickory crept into her mother's bedroom.

The bird became alarmed when it saw Hickory, and started flapping its wings. Hickory knew she had to act quickly otherwise the bird would wake Hilda.

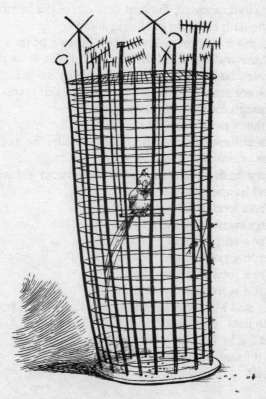

As fast as she could, she rushed over to the cage, opened the tiny door and grabbed hold of the bird. She rushed across the bedroom to make her escape.

Just as Hickory reached the bedroom door the yellow bird pecked her hand.

Hickory screamed and let go of it.

The bird flew round the room.

First it smashed into the dressing-table, then the bed-side lamp, then the wardrobe.

The noise woke Hilda.

'What's going on?' she asked. 'What?'

Hickory was panicking now.

'The bird has escaped!' cried Hickory. 'Help me catch it! Quick, Mum! Help me!'

But, at that moment, the bird flew out of the bedroom, down the hall, and into the living-room.

Now, the living-room had a hole in one of its walls. Most of the walls in Shadow Point had holes in by now. Some were large, the size of an oven or an armchair. Others were smaller. This one was small. But it was still large enough for the bird to fly through.

And that's exactly what happened!

The bird flew through the hole and into the endless corridors of Shadow Point.

Hickory rushed straight to Mercedes and explained what had happened.

'You're a fool!' cried Mercedes.

Hickory started crying.

'You're a stupid fool!'

Her crying got louder.

'You're a foolish stupid idiot!'

Her cries were now hysterical.

'Well,' said Mercedes satisfied, 'you know what you've got to do now, don't you?'

'What?' asked Hickory through her sobs.

'Find it,' said Mercedes.

'Find it?'

'Exactly! Find the bird. It must still be in Shadow Point. You know there's no escape. Find it. Search all of Shadow Point until you do. I want a glove made out of those magnificent yellow feathers.'

'If I find it,' said Hickory, 'will you love me for ever?'

'I don't know,' said Mercedes. 'You'll just have to find out.'

20

So Hickory filled a plastic bag with corned-beef sandwiches and tins of mandarins in syrup. Then she dressed

herself in her warmest clothes and set out to search the
endless corridors and stairways of Shadow Point.

The corridors were vast and cavernous, cold and full of

strange, frightening noises: screaming cats, crying babies and the scampering of rats.

Hickory started her search in the basement among the rumbling boilers and spiders. Gradually she made her way up, up through the floors of Shadow Point.

Meanwhile, Mrs Ice was getting thinner and thinner. Without Hickory, there was no one to do her shopping and she was feeling very ill.

She went into her son's bedroom and said, 'You'll have to get up, Mercedes. You'll have to get up and go to the shops. There's not a bite to eat.'

'But I don't want to eat,' said Mercedes. 'All I want is the yellow bird.'

'*You* might not want to eat,' said Mrs Ice angrily, 'but *I* do.'

Mercedes looked at his mother and smiled.

'Well,' he said, 'I'm not getting up. And that's that. I'm going to wait here until Hickory has searched all of Shadow Point.'

'But that could take ages!' cried Mrs Ice.

'It could,' agreed Mercedes.

21

Hilda Sparkle was moping round her flat and crying.

Crying non-stop.

She wanted her daughter back.

'Where is she?' cried Hilda. 'Where is my Hickory?'

She went into her daughter's bedroom and smelt the shoes Hickory used to wear.

'Oh, they smell of her!' cried Hilda. And she picked up some more shoes. 'They smell of her! They smell of her!'

Hilda spread all the shoes across the bed and touched them one at a time.

'Hickory has such tiny feet,' she said sadly. 'Such perfect little toes. And now all I've got left of her are these shoes.'

And she smelt another shoe.

And then another.

One morning, unable to bear her loneliness any longer, Hilda put all her daughter's shoes in a big black bag and went round to speak to Mrs Ice.

Mrs Ice opened the door, saw Hilda, then slammed the door shut in her face.

'Go away!' cried Mrs Ice.

'But I need to talk to someone,' said Hilda. 'I've lost my daughter and I'm all alone.'

'That's nothing,' said Mrs Ice. 'I'm starving. Now go away! I told you I don't want ever to talk to you again.'

'But why?' asked Hilda.

'We had an argument.'

'What about?' asked Hilda.

'Oh, I forget now,' replied Mrs Ice. 'All I know is I don't want to talk to you again.'

Hilda got to her knees and opened the letter-box.

'But I'm so lonely,' she said, sobbing.

On the other side of the door Mrs Ice got to *her* knees and looked through the letter-box.

'What's that big black bag you're carrying?' asked Mrs Ice.

'It's my Hickory's shoes,' said Hilda. 'It's all I've got left of her now.'

'All I can smell is sweaty feet,' said Mrs Ice. 'Now go away before you stink the place out.'

'But –'

'Go away!' screamed Mrs Ice.

Sadly, Hilda got to her feet and walked away from Mrs Ice's flat.

'Somewhere,' said Hilda, 'somewhere in Shadow Point is my little Hickory. I have to find her.'

So she tied the black bag of shoes round her neck and started searching the endless corridors of Shadow Point.

The black bag made walking difficult and sleeping impossible. But Hilda felt she had to wear it.

'It's my punishment,' Hilda kept saying. 'My punishment for scaring my daughter away.'

And she searched corridor after corridor, staircase after staircase, looking for her lost daughter.

Meanwhile, Hickory was searching for the yellow bird.
Sometimes she passed within a few feet of her mother. But
she never knew it. All the light bulbs had gone out and the
corridors of Shadow Point were as dark as night.

Back in her flat, Mrs Ice was getting hungry.

She searched through her cupboards and all she could find was an old sardine.

'I'd best cook it first,' said Mrs Ice, 'to kill all the germs!'

So she put the sardine in a frying-pan and covered it with fat.

She turned the gas on.

But she couldn't find a match to light the gas.

'Where are those matches?' she muttered. 'Where? I'm going to starve if I don't eat that sardine in a minute.'

She opened all the cupboards and all the drawers but still she couldn't find them.

She looked under the bed, in her wardrobe, in the dressing-table, under Mercedes's bed, in Mercedes's wardrobe, but still she couldn't find them.

'Where are they?' she muttered. 'Where are they?' Then she looked at Mercedes. 'Have you seen them?'

'Seen what?' asked Mercedes from his bed.

'The matches!' said Mrs Ice.

'No,' said Mercedes.

So, in desperation, Mrs Ice took a deep breath and opened the front door to her flat.

'I'm going to search Shadow Point!' she panted.

Mrs Ice squeezed and squeezed and squeezed through the doorway and into the darkness beyond . . .

— 24 —

For three days and three nights the corridors of Shadow Point were full of people looking for things:

Hickory was looking for the bird.

Hilda was looking for Hickory.

Mrs Ice was looking for a match.

The corridors echoed and reverberated with the patter of their footsteps.

Sometimes they passed very close to each other but never knew it.

And this went on for three days and nights until on the last day they all found what they wanted . . .

Somehow, they had all been drawn to the basement.

Hickory had heard the fluttering of wings and went inside. There, caught in the biggest spider's web she had ever seen, she found the yellow bird.

'At last!' said Hickory.

She rushed forward and disentangled the pretty bird from the web.

'Now Mercedes will love me,' she said.

And she kissed the bird's hard beak.

At that moment Hilda rushed into the basement. She had heard Hickory's voice from outside.

'Hickory!' cried Hilda.

'Mummy!' cried Hickory. 'What's that bag doing round your neck?'

At that moment Mrs Ice came into the basement. She had heard Hilda's voice from outside. She looked at Hickory and Hilda.

'Have either of you got a match?' she asked.

'Yes,' said Hilda. And gave her a box full of them.

They all looked at each other and smiled.

'Are you talking to me now?' asked Hilda.

Mrs Ice was so hungry she answered without thinking.

'Yes,' she said.

Hilda smiled.

'We've all found what we were after,' said Hilda. 'I've found Hickory.'

'And I've found the bird,' said Hickory.

'And I've found a match,' said Mrs Ice.

'Light one,' said Hilda. 'There's plenty of them. Let's have some light when we go back home. I want to see where I'm going from now on.'

So Mrs Ice struck a match.

There was a loud explosion.

And Shadow Point fell down like a pack of cards . . .

— 26 —

Rubble.

Nothing but rubble and dust.

Rubble and dust and the smell of gas.

When Mrs Ice struck the match it set off a chain of endless gas explosions. (She had left the gas on when she went looking for the matches, don't forget.)

Shadow Point collapsed in ten seconds.

Concrete walls caved in on concrete walls.

Thirty-four floors became one floor.

BANG! went Shadow Point.

And then . . .

Rubble.

Nothing but rubble and dust.

Rubble and dust and Mercedes Ice.

Rubble and dust and Hickory Sparkle.

Mercedes Ice was still in his bed. He looked at Hickory Sparkle.

Hickory Sparkle struggled to her feet and looked at Mercedes Ice.

Both of them were bruised and covered in dirt.

Mercedes looked at the wilderness around him.

'Did you find my bird?' he asked.

'It must be buried in the rubble,' said Hickory. 'I'm sorry.'

And Mercedes started to cry.

And as he cried, so his tears seemed to give colour back to the world. At least, that's what Mercedes thought.

'My tears are magical!' he cried.

'Stop talking rubbish!' said Hickory. 'The heat from the explosion has melted the snow! That's all! It has nothing to do with your stupid tears!'

Then she looked at the ruins and saw something gleaming.

It was a tin helmet painted gold.

'Look!' cried Hickory. 'Look!'

Mercedes looked at the golden helmet.

'What is it?' he asked.

'It's my crown,' said Hickory. 'I am now the Cobweb Queen.'

And, as if to prove her point, spiders started to scamper out of the rubble and cluster round her feet.

'So what am I?' asked Mercedes. 'I have no kingdom. Everything has turned to rubble and dust.'

'Exactly!' said Hickory. 'You have nothing and I have everything.'

'But what shall I do?' asked Mercedes.

Hickory put the golden helmet on her head.

Spiders started to climb up her legs.

'I've got nothing,' said Mercedes.

Hickory looked at Mercedes.

'Listen,' she said. 'Will you serve me for the rest of my life?'

'Yes,' said Mercedes softly.

'Will you do everything I say?'

'Yes,' said Mercedes softly.

'Will you be my slave in the Cobweb Kingdom?'

'Yes,' said Mercedes.

Then he looked at Hickory and asked:

'If I do all this . . . if I serve you and do everything you say and be your slave . . . if I do all this . . . will you love me?'

Hickory thought for a while.

'I don't know,' she said. 'You'll just have to find out . . .'

And then, suddenly, the yellow bird rose from the rubble between them and, flapping its wings for all it was worth, flew to the blue sky above.

READ MORE IN PUFFIN

For children of all ages, Puffin represents quality and variety – the very best in publishing today around the world.

For complete information about books available from Puffin – and Penguin – and how to order them, contact us at the appropriate address below. Please note that for copyright reasons the selection of books varies from country to country.

On the worldwide web: www.puffin.co.uk

In the United Kingdom: Please write to *Dept. EP, Penguin Books Ltd, Bath Road, Harmondsworth, West Drayton, Middlesex UB7 ODA*

In the United States: Please write to *Consumer Sales, Penguin USA, P.O. Box 999, Dept. 17109, Bergenfield, New Jersey 07621-0120*. VISA and MasterCard holders call 1-800-253-6476 to order Penguin titles

In Canada: Please write to *Penguin Books Canada Ltd, 10 Alcorn Avenue, Suite 300, Toronto, Ontario M4V 3B2*

In Australia: Please write to *Penguin Books Australia Ltd, P.O. Box 257, Ringwood, Victoria 3134*

In New Zealand: Please write to *Penguin Books (NZ) Ltd, Private Bag 102902, North Shore Mail Centre, Auckland 10*

In India: Please write to *Penguin Books India Pvt Ltd, 706 Eros Apartments, 56 Nehru Place, New Delhi 110 019*

In the Netherlands: Please write to *Penguin Books Netherlands bv, Postbus 3507, NL-1001 AH Amsterdam*

In Germany: Please write to *Penguin Books Deutschland GmbH, Metzlerstrasse 26, 60594 Frankfurt am Main*

In Spain: Please write to *Penguin Books S. A., Bravo Murillo 19, 1° B, 28015 Madrid*

In Italy: Please write to *Penguin Italia s.r.l., Via Felice Casati 20, I–20124 Milano*

In France: Please write to *Penguin France S. A., 17 rue Lejeune, F–31000 Toulouse*

In Japan: Please write to *Penguin Books Japan, Ishikiribashi Building, 2–5–4, Suido, Bunkyo-ku, Tokyo 112*

In South Africa: Please write to *Longman Penguin Southern Africa (Pty) Ltd, Private Bag X08, Bertsham 2013*